JUST iMAGiNE
A MORE BEAUTIFUL WORLD

BY CHRISTINE MCDONALD
ILLUSTRATED BY JULENE EWERT

Printed in the
United States of America
First Edition
Just Imagine a More Beautiful World
Summary: Children's story of creating their own beautiful world

ISBN: 979-8-9854448-3-4

DEDiCATiON

This book is inspired by my first day of school which was overwhelming.
All I wanted to do was crawl under my desk. I reimagined the day starting with everyone
crawling under their desk and the story took off from there.

To everyone starting a new day of school, a new project, or a new job.

Life is full of challenges and surprises! But here is to the best of beginnings,

belonging and making the world a better place.

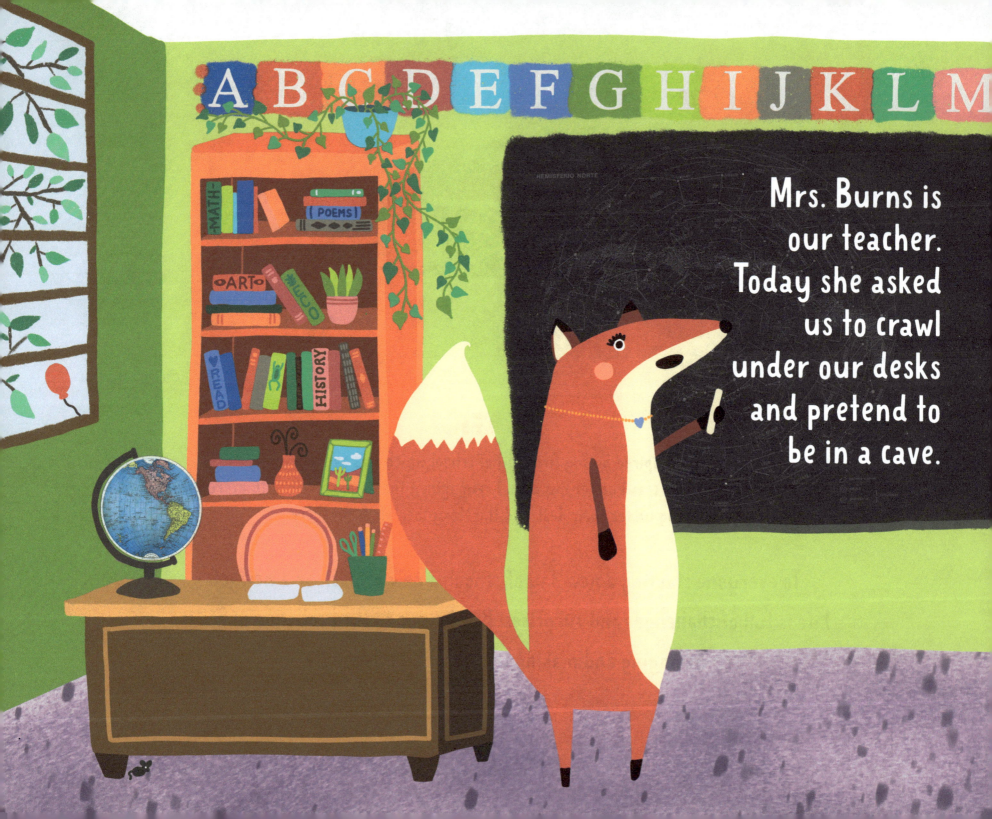

Mrs. Burns is our teacher. Today she asked us to crawl under our desks and pretend to be in a cave.

She handed out cardboard. "You are going to make your own world," she told us.

Then she gave us soft red hearts to sit on.

"The safest place to BE is in your heart," she said.

Just imagine a world
where everyone knows
where their heart is!

Mrs Burns told us our world is timeless. "You have all the time in the world to make it," she said,

Our imaginations went wild,

before anyone
picked up a crayon.

Mrs. Burns reminded us to make a door.

"Sometimes you may forget your way, and you will

always have a way back to your heart," she said.

Our whole class started laughing, each enjoying our own world.

Everyone had so much fun.

We played our way
through the day together,

making the most
beautiful world where
everyone belonged.

By the end of the day we all knew we could be whatever we wanted to be...

...because we are always at home in our world!

YES, JUST
iMAGiNE!

ARIES

LION

LION

Regulus

LITTLE LION

EXTRA CAKES

JUST iMAGiNE
CRAFT PAGE

Imagine a world where everyone feels at home in their heart.

What does your heart tell you is possible?

Put your hand on your heart.

Feel it beating. What does it feel like?

Imagine the earth has a heart beating with yours.

Feeling your heart and the heart of the earth.

Bun Bun is here to help you get started.

1. Draw a heart in the middle of a circle shaped like the earth. You can also use a paper plate. What does your beautiful heart want to express?

2. Using crayons, colored pencils or any art medium you like color the earth and then color your heart.

NOW, JUST IMAGINE HOW MANY OTHER WAYS YOU CAN MAKE A BEAUTIFUL WORLD.

3. Now turn the paper over. Imagine three things that bring you joy and can make a more beautiful world.
Write, draw, color, sing or dance your beautiful heart.

Zip on over to Christinemcdonald.net/Imagine for a downloadable craft page.

ABOUT THE AUTHOR

Christine McDonald is delighted you are holding this children's book and hopes you will be inspired to create a more beautiful world. She is a mom, lover of the earth, animals and small green wild things and works as a soil scientist. She lives in Pullman Washington with her husband and writes poetry that brings alive her love and wonder for life. Other books by Christine are My Two Mothers, A Collection of Poetry and Prose, and Where Everything Wild Has a Home, Wild Poems. You can learn more about her work at christinemcdonald.net

ABOUT THE iLLUSTRATOR

Julene Ewert is a visual artist and storyteller working in painting, illustration, and collage. Her art is whimsical in spirit, and expresses an honest and a playful curiosity of the world. This is her third book. Her artwork can be found in galleries, gift shops and homes globally. She lives her passion in an undiscovered part of the beautiful Pacific Northwest. juleneewert.com